Also by Jane Buchanan

Gratefully Yours
Hank's Story

The Berry-Picking Man

The Berry-Picking Man

Jane Buchanan
Pictures by Leslie Bowman

Farrar, Straus and Giroux
New York

Library of Congress Cataloging-in-Publication Data
Buchanan, Jane, date–
    The berry-picking man / Jane Buchanan ; pictures by
  Leslie Bowman.— 1st ed.
        p.   cm.
    Summary: Nine-year-old Meggie resents spending time with a
  strange, smelly old man who calls her mother whenever he needs
  a ride, but when Christmas finds him in the hospital she knows
  what she must do.
    ISBN 0-374-40610-3
    [1. Empathy—Fiction.   2. Old age—Fiction.   3. Family life—
  Fiction.   4. Berries—Fiction.   5. Christmas—Fiction.]   I. Bowman,
  Leslie W., ill.   II. Title.

PZ7.B877135 Be 2003
[Fic]—dc21

                                                    2001033794

For Fred

The Berry-Picking Man

ONE

Meggie was up in her room reading when she heard the phone ring. She held her breath and listened.

"Yes, Sam!" Mama shouted. She was downstairs in her darkroom with the door closed, and still Meggie could hear her loud and clear.

"Shoot!" Meggie said. This was the fourth time in two weeks. She dropped her book and scrambled under her bed. Maybe Mama wouldn't be able to find her.

"Yes, Sam!" Mama shouted again. She must have hung up the phone. Meggie heard the darkroom door open and close.

"Meggie?" Mama called.

Meggie moved farther under the bed and scrunched up so Mama couldn't see any body parts sticking out. She heard Mama's footsteps on the stairs.

"Meggie?"

In the hall. "Meggie?"

At her door. "Meggie," Mama said. From her hiding place, Meggie could see Mama still wiping print-processing chemicals from her hands. "Get out from under that bed and put on your shoes. I'll get the kettle."

Meggie groaned. How could Mama always tell?

"Do I have to?" she said. "I was reading." That was one of the best excuses you could use with Mama, but not when it came to Old Sam.

"Yes, you have to," Mama said.

Meggie groaned again and slid out from under the bed. She brushed the dust bunnies off her shorts and T-shirt and out of her hair. It wasn't fair. Why couldn't one of her sisters go for once? It was the curse of being the "baby." Reenie and Lissa were too grown up to be seen with their mother, but Meggie was only nine.

"I don't see why I have to go with you. Why can't you pick up Old Sam by yourself? You're the one who said yes."

But Mama only said, "Meggie," in that way she had where she held on to the "ie" and drew it out like a warning growl. And Meggie knew it was time to put on her shoes and get into the car.

Mama got the big blue speckled canning kettle out of the basement and put it in the back seat. Meggie sat in front so Mama could catch the full force of her sulking face. If there was one thing Meggie hated about summer, it was Old Sam.

TWO

Meggie couldn't remember ever meeting Old Sam. It seemed to her he had always been there, in his dirty torn undershirt and baggy green pants. He had white whiskers that covered his cheeks and chin like dandelion fuzz, and his hair stuck up from his head in a tangle. He wore black-framed glasses that were taped together on one side at the temple. He always had a scowl on his face.

Mama had a photograph over her computer of Old Sam standing in front of their garage, squinting into the sun, holding their cat Millicent when she was just a kitten. Millie was old

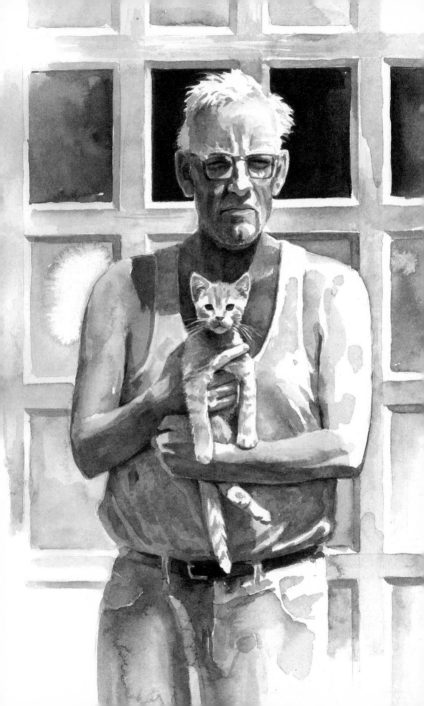

now, but as far as Meggie could see, Old Sam hadn't even changed his clothes since then.

Like most of Mama's work, the photograph was black and white. "Not black and white," Mama told Meggie once. "Nothing's black and white. Look closely. It's degrees of gray; shadow and light. That's what I love about photography. It's like life." But it looked pretty black and white to Meggie.

Mama said Old Sam just walked into church one morning out of nowhere. Right in the middle of the sermon, he marched up to the front row and plunked himself down. He sat there with his hand cupped around his ear. Every now and then he'd say, "What's that?" in a loud voice. Then he'd fiddle with his hearing aid until it started to squeal.

Later they found out Old Sam had spent twenty-five years in a psychiatric hospital. His brother put him there, Mama said. Sam said his brother just didn't like him, that he'd never been crazy. But Mama said, if he wasn't crazy when he went in, he had learned a lot of crazy behavior by the time the hospital's funding got cut and it couldn't afford to keep patients who could make it on their own. Meggie guessed in Sam's case "make it on their own" meant he could afford to rent a room over the dry cleaner's—if nothing else, his brother had left him lots of money when he died.

Old Sam talked to himself—loudly. He got too close and talked about things polite people didn't talk about. He made people uncomfortable. It was as though after twenty-five years in the hospital he had forgotten all the rules about how to behave. Or maybe he'd never learned them, and that was why he was in the hospital to begin with.

Once Meggie asked Mama why Old Sam had ended up in their town, but Mama didn't know. "Just luck, I guess," she said. Yeah, Meggie thought. Bad luck.

To the kids in town, Old Sam was the berry-picking man. Every year, from June to September, he went out into the woods and fields around town and picked wild fruit. He picked strawberries and blueberries, blackberries and raspberries. And grapes—delicious, purple fox grapes that were sweet and juicy and stained your lips and fingers when you ate them.

Then the phone would ring.

"Nan?" That was all he'd say when you picked up the phone. Nan was Mama's name.

"Nan?" he'd say, and whoever answered it would go and get Mama.

When Mama got on the phone, he'd say, "I'm at the gas station. Come get me." And he'd hang up. Never a hello or goodbye or a please or thank you. Meggie knew, because he talked so loud she could hear him clear across the room.

Then Mama would get the kettle and take Meggie away from whatever she was doing, and they would go to the gas station to pick up Old Sam.

"Why don't you just say no?" Meggie asked once. "Why can't he call someone else?"

"He does call other people," Mama said. "But it's our turn. We can't leave him standing at the gas station with pails of rotting fruit."

I could, Meggie thought. But she didn't say it out loud. It seemed to her it was always their turn.

THREE

Mama had barely stopped the car when Old Sam came storming over with his strawberries. "What took you so long?" he demanded to know. As if Mama didn't have anything else to do!

"We got here as soon as we could," Mama said. Then, to change the subject, she said, "Oh, what lovely berries, Sam."

"Five quarts," Old Sam said proudly, holding up two tin pails for Mama and Meggie to see. Mama got out the kettle, and he poured the berries into it. They made a drumming sound as they hit the bottom.

"Taste them," Old Sam ordered.

Mama picked up a couple and popped them into her mouth. She smiled as though she'd never tasted anything so wonderful. "Try one, Meggie," she said.

Meggie could have spit. The last thing she wanted to do was eat berries that had had Sam's dirty old fingers all over them. But Mama was waiting, and so was Old Sam. She ate one. It was good. It really was. Sweet and fresh. The seeds crunched between her teeth. But still, that they hadn't been washed yet made her gag a little when she swallowed. "Mmm," she said with a forced smile.

"Are they sweet enough?" he asked.

"Yes, Sam," Mama said. "They're fine." She always said they were fine, whether they really were or not. Not just to be polite, but because if she said they needed sugar or something, Old Sam got upset.

"It makes him happy to pick them," she told Meggie. "That's the important thing."

Sam got into the front, next to Mama. Meggie took a big gulp of fresh air and climbed into the back. She rolled down the window and stuck her head out. Mama was scowling at her through the rearview mirror, but Meggie didn't care. Mama couldn't expect her to breathe in Old Sam all the way home in a hot car. Old Sam smelled bad, really bad. He didn't wash very often to begin with, and picking all those berries was hard work, so he had sweat a lot. Meggie wondered whether his mother had nagged him when he was a kid about washing behind his ears and using soap, the way her mother nagged her. She wondered when it was that he had stopped washing.

Sam was talking to Mama in his too-loud voice. He was kind of deaf, so Meggie guessed it was hard to hear himself talk. And he talked a lot. Maybe not many people would listen to him the way Mama did, so he had to get in as much as he could when he had the chance. He talked about how many berries he'd picked so far that season. He always knew how many quarts and pints. And he talked about astronomy. He knew all about the stars and planets. Then he got quiet for a minute—or as quiet as possible, considering you could hear his breathing as far away as Pluto.

Meggie put her hands in front of her face and made a frame with her fingers. She peered through it, looking at Old Sam as though she were seeing him through her mother's camera.

"It's a matter of learning how to see," Mama always said about her work.

"How can I learn to see if I don't have a camera of my own?" Meggie had asked. So Mama had shown her how to make her hands into a viewfinder.

"A camera is a big responsibility," Mama had said.

All of a sudden, Old Sam turned and stared at Meggie through his thick glasses, which looked as if he never cleaned them. Meggie quickly dropped her hands.

"Dear girl," he said in a voice rough as sandpaper. Then, to Mama, "She's my favorite child."

Meggie smiled until her cheeks hurt and

looked out the window. Turn around, she willed him. Please turn around. But he didn't.

"I like you, Meggie," he said. "Do you like me?"

Meggie always hated it when he asked her that. What could she say? No, I hate you? Go away and never come back? She could hear Mama now! So she just kept smiling like an idiot.

Old Sam put his fingers to his lips and blew Meggie a kiss. Meggie shuddered. Finally Mama distracted him by saying, "She's a good girl, isn't she, Sam?"

He turned around then and started telling Mama about the ocean cruise he was going on in November. That was one of the weird things about Old Sam. He lived in a dirty little room over the dry cleaner's on Main Street. He dressed like a bum. But he wasn't poor. Every year he went on cruises around the world to see eclipses and comets and meteor showers and such. He had a niece who lived far enough away that she didn't have to smell him. She arranged it all for him.

Papa had said, "Imagine saving your whole life to go on a cruise only to find yourself in a cabin next to Sam." Meggie leaned out the window and took another gulp of fresh air. She hoped those cruise ships had lots of windows.

FOUR

Meggie crossed her fingers and wished as hard as she could that Mama would drop Old Sam off at his room, as she usually did, instead of bringing him back to their house for one of his disgusting peanut butter and cheese and pickle and jelly sandwiches.

It didn't work.

"Shall I leave you at your room, Sam?" she asked.

"No," he said. That was it. Just "No."

Meggie couldn't believe the way this day was going. What had she done to deserve it? She had just been sitting in her room, reading a book. And where were her big sisters, Reenie and

Lissa? Probably at the pool with their friends. Not that Mama would have asked them to go with her. That was Meggie's privilege.

Meggie slumped down in her seat and glared at her mother through the rearview mirror. Her mother scowled back. Why she worried about being rude to Old Sam was beyond Meggie's comprehension. As if he spent his spare time reading Miss Manners!

When they got home, Papa was outside mowing the lawn, a task he usually saved for Saturdays instead of his afternoon off—he must have known Old Sam was coming. Reenie and Lissa were still invisible. They'd stay that way until Old Sam was gone, too. Meggie would bet on it. She knew her mother wouldn't let her leave the room, either. Mama wasn't afraid of Old Sam, but she didn't want to be alone with him. Before Papa had told him not to, Old Sam used to follow Mama around the kitchen and touch her cheek. Meggie's too. That was all he did, just touch their cheeks. And Mama would say, "Imagine never having anyone to hug you, Meggie." But Mama didn't like it, and neither did Meggie. So finally Papa told Sam that if he wanted to keep coming over, he had to stop. And he did. But Mama still felt better when someone else was around.

Meggie started in washing the strawberries and hulling them while Mama made Sam a sandwich.

"Something to drink, Sam?" Mama asked.

"Water," Sam said. "Lots of ice. Fresh lemon juice. No sugar."

Meggie rolled her eyes. Leave it to Sam. He couldn't even drink something normal. No soda for Old Sam. And he certainly wouldn't eat anything like a hot dog or a hamburger, or even a bacon, lettuce, and tomato sandwich. He was a vegetarian, which meant he didn't eat animal flesh. Actually, if she let herself think about it, Meggie could understand that. But she tried not to think about it too much, because she couldn't imagine life without BLTs.

Meggie popped a strawberry into her mouth.

"Leave some for the jam," Mama said.

"I only ate one," Meggie said. "There's a bazillion here."

"They'll make good jam," Old Sam said. "They're sweet. The sweetest this year. You won't even need sugar."

Meggie just kept hulling strawberries. Since wild strawberries are tiny, about the size of a peanut M&M, five quarts meant a lot of tops to be removed. She pulled up a stool and perched there while she worked.

Mama finished making the sandwich. She filled a glass with ice, squeezed a lemon into it, and added cold water. Meggie's mouth puckered at the thought of it. But she supposed the sour lemon would wash away the taste of the sandwich pretty fast.

For the second time that day, she found herself thinking about Old Sam's past. When was it that he started eating like this? His mother wouldn't have made such sandwiches for him, would she? Meggie would never ask, but she did wonder.

She looked at him. There were bits of cheese and smears of peanut butter stuck to the stubble

on his chin. She tried to imagine him in black and white—shades of gray—framed in the rectangle of her fingers. "That's a photograph," Mama would say.

Mama handed Sam a napkin. He didn't use it. He was fingering the cube puzzle Lissa had gotten for her birthday. It had four plastic cubes, with different colors on each side. The idea was to line them up so all four had the same color showing on the same side. When you were done, you'd have a tower of blocks with all the reds, all the blues, all the whites, and all the yellows on their own side. The whole family had taken a try at it, but no one had been able to do the puzzle. Meggie had gotten the blues together once, but the other colors had been all mixed up.

Between bites of his sandwich and swallows of his lemon water, Old Sam looked at the blocks. He held each one up and turned it around. Before Meggie had finished hulling another quart of strawberries, Old Sam had figured out that puzzle. She couldn't believe it. Mama had said he was a genius, but this was amazing. Reenie and Lissa weren't going to believe it.

"You should take a picture, Mama," Meggie said, "so we can show everybody."

Mama laughed. "That's terrific, Sam," she said. But Old Sam didn't seem to think it was such a big deal. He dropped the blocks on the table with a clatter and went back to his sandwich. Rats, she thought, now her sisters would never believe her.

"Take me home," Sam said when he had finished eating. Not even a "please." Meggie would never be allowed to talk to Mama like that. For someone so smart, Old Sam sure didn't act it. He was like a three-year-old when he wanted something.

Meggie could feel Mama's eyes boring into the back of her head, but she was not going to turn around and catch her mother's "get in the car we have to drive Sam downtown" look straight in her face. It worked. Mama and Sam left without her.

She should have been happy, but she wasn't. She felt guilty. It wasn't fair. Even when Mama lost, she won.

FIVE

Miraculously, Reenie and Lissa showed up as soon as Old Sam left. Maybe they had Old Sam radar.

"Where have you guys been?" Meggie said.

"Around," said Reenie.

"None of your business," Lissa said.

Lissa poured a glass of iced tea and sat down at the table. She picked up one of the blocks Old Sam had been fiddling with. "What are these doing out?" she said. "They're mine."

Lissa was tall and thin, with hair the color of dark chocolate. It was long and fine, and she wore it pulled back tightly into a ponytail that hung to her waist. It was the kind of hair you saw on models in magazines, Meggie thought—the kind of hair she, with her short spiky cowlicks, would never have. She ignored the comment.

"Sam solved the puzzle," she said.

Lissa made a noise with her tongue that sounded like something between disgust and disbelief.

"Really," Meggie said. "Ask Mama. It took him about three minutes. I swear."

"Three minutes?" said Reenie. "Wow!" Reenie was the oldest. She was shorter and softer than Lissa, with blond curls that frizzed out from her head. She tried to control them with headbands and various kinds of goop, but they were always springing loose by afternoon, adding an inch or two of fuzz to her height. Meggie thought that when the sun hit her just right, she seemed to have a halo. Not that Reenie's behavior was particularly angelic.

"Yeah," said Meggie. "I wanted Mama to take a picture to show everybody, but he dropped it."

Reenie picked out a strawberry and popped it into her mouth. "That's so weird," she said.

"Maybe you have to be crazy to solve it. That's why nobody else could even come close."

"I don't know," said Meggie. "Mama always says he's a math genius."

"Who cares," said Lissa. "It's just a stupid puzzle." She put the block she was holding on the table and pushed out her chair. She grabbed a handful of strawberries that Meggie had hulled and crammed them into her mouth on her way out the door.

"What's her problem?" Meggie said.

Reenie shrugged and began hulling strawberries, using her long fingernails to pluck off the tops, instead of a paring knife.

Meggie admired Reenie's nails. They were like small daggers at the tips of her fingers. She didn't paint them the way Lissa did. But Meggie had seen her dismember a mosquito with them, leg by leg, wing by wing. It was gross, but impressive! And now she was using the same razorlike precision on the strawberries. She obviously didn't mind that her nails were being stained red with the juice.

Meggie, on the other hand, bit her nails. Every one of them was a raggedy mess. She even bit around her nails. Mama had tried painting them with that disgusting-tasting stuff you put on little kids' thumbs to prevent thumb sucking, but it didn't work. Nothing worked. Meggie was a hopeless nail biter. She would never be able to hull a strawberry without a knife, much less pick apart a mosquito.

She was chewing a loose piece of skin on her right thumb when she heard Mama's car in the driveway. She took her thumb out of her mouth and shoved her hand in her pocket.

"What's for dinner?" Lissa asked when Mama came up the steps.

"Pizza," said Mama, "and strawberry shortcake for dessert."

"I thought the strawberries were for jam," Meggie called from the kitchen. She heard Mama plunk down onto one of the wicker rockers on the back porch.

"They were," she said, "but it's too hot to make jam. I'll just throw together some shortcake and be done with it. I bought some whipping cream after I dropped off Sam."

"Cool," said Reenie. She decapitated another strawberry. "I'll whip the cream."

"I'll make the shortcake," Meggie said. She was still feeling guilty for making Mama drive Sam home alone.

"Thanks," Mama said, coming in from the porch. "I'll have a glass of lemonade—with sugar!" She opened the refrigerator and took out the pitcher, which stood on a shelf next to a bowl of uneaten strawberries covered with a layer of white fuzz. Good thing Sam hadn't seen that!

"Isn't strawberry season almost over?" Meggie asked.

"It won't matter," said Lissa, rolling her eyes in disgust. "It'll be blueberries next."

"Then blackberries," said Reenie. "And raspberries." She licked her lips and slurped in anticipation.

"Then grapes," said Mama.

"Mmm," said Meggie. In spite of herself, she did love grape season. She couldn't help it. She always looked forward to Mama's grape chiffon pie. And the jam was like nothing you could buy in the store—dark and rich and tangy.

Mama laughed. "So you won't go hiding on me when it's time to pick up Sam during grape season?"

"I didn't say that," Meggie said. "Besides," she added, sensing the time was right, "how come I'm always the one who has to go? Why not Reenie or Lissa?"

"Yeah, right," said Lissa.

Reenie just showed her claws.

"Because," said Mama, "you're the only one who will."

As if she had any choice, Meggie thought. She was too young to stay home alone and too young to do anything with Lissa and Reenie, so she was always there when Sam called. She folded her arms across her chest and sighed angrily. It wasn't fair. She hated being the baby.

SIX

One thing Meggie liked about summer was helping Mama in her darkroom. She mixed chemicals, wiped down the counters, hung prints to dry on the line over the developing trays. She loved the way the darkroom smelled—like Mama—and she never ceased to be amazed when the images appeared on the blank pieces of photographic paper.

"I wish I had a real camera of my own," Meggie said for the millionth time as she was clipping prints to the line one day.

"You will," Mama said. She was focused on her enlarger, not on Meggie, Meggie could tell.

"When I'm older," Meggie said, finishing the

thought for her mother, who, it seemed, couldn't be bothered.

"Mmm," Mama said distractedly.

Meggie couldn't figure out why it made her so cross. Her mother was often preoccupied when she was in the darkroom. But this time Meggie didn't care. She opened the door and stomped out, leaving her mother struggling to protect her precious paper from the light.

"No one ever takes me seriously around here," Meggie muttered as she slammed the door to her bedroom and flopped facedown on her bed.

After a while, Mama came up and knocked on her door. "Meggie?"

"What?" Meggie snapped.

"Are you all right?"

"I'm fine," she said.

The door opened, and Mama stuck her head in. "Can we talk?" she said.

Meggie shrugged.

"You left in kind of a hurry," Mama said.

"Sorry," Meggie said.

"Hey, only one sheet of paper lost," said

Mama. She brushed Meggie's hair out of her face. Meggie inhaled the sharp scent of fixer.

"Well, anyway, I'm sorry," Meggie said. "But it makes me angry when you don't listen to me."

"You want to take photographs," Mama said. They were photographs to Mama, not pictures. Photographs, she always said, are art.

"Yes," said Meggie.

"A real camera is a big responsibility," Mama said, looking around Meggie's room, which was, as usual, piled with stuff.

Meggie knew her mother was thinking that she couldn't even be trusted to take care of her laundry. "It doesn't have to be fancy," she said. "It doesn't even have to be new."

Mama smiled, and Meggie could tell she was looking for a way to tell her she wasn't old enough. She shrugged. "It's no big deal," she said, trying to sound as though she meant it. She rolled back onto her stomach to end the conversation.

She was still fuming that afternoon when she heard Mama ask Old Sam to dig up a tree stump in the backyard for her. Meggie couldn't believe it. Picking him up at the gas station was bad enough, but having him there for hours, digging and sweating and snacking in the kitchen, was too much. Old Sam was strong, but it was a big stump. It was going to take forever.

"It makes him feel useful," said Mama. "And I need the stump removed. It won't be so bad."

Yeah, right, Meggie thought. For you, maybe.

Meggie had taken to hiding whenever she saw Sam coming near the house: under the dining-room table, where she was concealed by the tablecloth; in the cubby hole under the stairs; in the attic, among the old trunks and toys and furniture. Sam started calling her Heidi. It made her feel guilty, but not guilty enough to stop hiding.

While Sam was outside, she phoned her best friend, Jolene. She and Jo had been friends since preschool.

"Why don't you just tell your mom to stop letting him come over?" Jo asked.

"It wouldn't work," Meggie said. "You don't

understand." Not that Meggie did either, really. But she knew her mother felt Old Sam needed her. And she also knew Mama was probably right.

"Where's Heidi?" he said to Mama when he came in. He said it loud, so Meggie would hear him.

"I don't know, Sam," Mama said, even though she knew perfectly well.

"She's my favorite," Sam said.

"She is a good girl," Mama answered. But Meggie didn't feel good.

"It's no fair," Meggie said after Mama had returned Old Sam to his room.

"What's no fair?" Mama asked.

"No one else feels guilty about Old Sam. Daddy doesn't."

"No," said Mama.

"Reenie and Lissa don't."

"No," said Mama.

"Reverend Wallace does, but that's her job."

Mama laughed. "True," she said.

"So how come we do?" Meggie said.

Mama hugged her. "It's called empathy," she said. "This being able to feel other people's hurts. To see the world through their lens." She hugged Meggie again. "It's a gift, I guess," she said. "Or a curse, more like." She laughed again, but Meggie didn't think it was funny.

SEVEN

"Here he comes!" Reenie shouted.

It was the first Sunday in September, and Reenie was the lookout. Every Sunday it was someone different. The lookout had to watch for Old Sam and warn the rest of the kids when he was headed for the stairs to go down for coffee hour.

"Quick!" Lissa whispered loudly. "Run!"

All of them, girls and boys both, tore off down the stairs and hid in the girls' room. There was no lock, so as many as could fit pushed their backs up against the door to stop Old Sam from getting in. They stayed there, holding their breaths, waiting to hear Old Sam shuffle past.

Sam's step was heavy and uneven, and the

floorboards creaked under his weight. He was halfway down the hall when he stopped and came back to the girls' room door. He rattled the knob.

The kids looked at each other wide-eyed. Lissa was trying not to laugh. Meggie hoped she wouldn't, because if she did, they would all start, and it would be hopeless.

"I know you're in there," Sam said. They could hear him breathing. "Heidi?" he called.

"Heidi?" Lissa whispered. "Who's Heidi?" She looked as if she was about to burst out laughing, and Meggie wondered how she could not know he was talking about her.

"Shh!" said Meggie, putting her finger to her lips. This was just a joke to Lissa. To all of them, Meggie thought. None of them had to worry as much as she did. None of them was Old Sam's favorite. She squeezed her eyes shut to stop the tears from coming. What was so special about her, anyway? Why had Old Sam picked her? It wasn't because she was the youngest.

Finally, they heard him shuffle off, and they relaxed their hold on the door. After a while, Lissa opened the door a crack and peeked out. "All clear," she said. She flung the door wide and they burst into the hallway, gulping in the fresh air.

All except Meggie. She stuck her head out of the doorway and looked both ways. She didn't want to run into Sam. She didn't want to run into anyone. She felt ashamed. And she felt angry. She shouldn't have to feel guilty about not liking Old Sam. No one else did. Not even her mother really liked him. She slunk out the back door of the church and started slowly home.

It stank, that was all. She wished Old Sam had never come to their town. She wished he was still in the loony bin, where he belonged. And she wished her mother didn't have to be so nice!

Heidi! She kicked a stone on the sidewalk. She kicked it again, hard. It bounced on the concrete and rolled into the street, ricocheting off a passing car. The driver scowled and said something Meggie couldn't hear through the rolled-up window. Her ears burned, and she wanted to cry.

She walked faster. She couldn't wait to get home. She wanted to crawl into bed and pull the covers over her head and never come out again. Heidi. That's who she was, all right.

She heard footsteps behind her, but she didn't turn around. "Meggie?" It was Mama. There was an edge of concern in her voice. "Are you all right?"

"I'm fine," she snapped, and began walking faster.

Meggie shook her head. The last thing she wanted to do was walk with the person whose fault all this was. Besides, she didn't want to talk to anyone. And she certainly didn't want to hear a lecture about Old Sam. Why couldn't they all just leave her alone? She kept walking. She could hear Lissa and Reenie talking and laughing behind her. She wanted to spit.

When she got home, she was tired and hot. Sweat dripped beneath her church dress in tickly little rivers.

She went up to her room and closed the door. She peeled off her dress, tossing it across the room, where it landed in a heap by her closet. She tugged on a pair of shorts and a tank top and flopped down on her bed.

Meggie picked up the book she was reading and tried not to think about her lousy day. Absentmindedly, she chewed on a thumbnail while she read. She was engrossed in her book, thinking how wonderful it would be to escape to another world through a "wrinkle in time," when there was a knock on her door.

"Shoot," she thought. It was Mama. She could tell by the knock. Her sisters always barged right in, and her father knocked once, then opened the door. Only Mama waited outside for her to answer.

"Meggie?" Mama said.

"What?" She was surprised by how harsh her voice sounded.

"May I come in?"

"Suit yourself," Meggie said.

Slowly the door opened, and Mama peeked around it. "Hey, cutie," she said. She was smiling, but the lines between her eyebrows had gotten deeper, the way they did when she was worried. She picked up Meggie's dress and dropped it in her hamper.

Mama sat on the bed for a moment, not saying anything. Every bit of her smelled like darkroom chemicals: her hair, her hands, her clothes. It was a smell Meggie took comfort in—most of the time. Mama kissed Meggie's head and said, "You are a very special girl, you know."

Meggie felt the tears starting in the corners of her eyes. "Everyone hates me." She was sobbing now.

Mama looked surprised. She put her arm around Meggie. "Nobody hates you," she said. "Whatever gave you that idea?"

She couldn't explain it. Maybe it was just that she was ashamed of herself—for hiding from Sam, for making fun of him. Maybe she knew, deep down, that Mama should be as disappointed in her as she was in herself. But she didn't say so; couldn't say so.

"Old Sam follows me everywhere and calls me

Heidi," she said, sniffing loudly and ignoring her mother's question. "I can't help it. I don't like to be around him."

Mama sighed. "Poor old man," she said.

"Poor old man?" Meggie said. She was angry now. "What about me? Why is it always about Sam? Why do I have to be nice and considerate and polite and no one else does?" She pushed her mother's arm away. "It's not my fault he doesn't have anyone to hug him!"

"No," said Mama. "And I don't ever want you to feel you have to hug or touch anyone you don't want to. Your body is yours. You have the right to decide who can touch you and who can't." Mama sighed. "I wasn't trying to tell you that you should let Old Sam hug you. Heaven knows, I don't let him hug me, either. I'm just thinking about how sad and lonely it must be to be him, that's all. I guess that's why I keep taking his berries—even when we end up throwing half of them in the compost heap!"

Meggie wiped the tears off her cheeks with the

hem of her tank top. She sniffed. "I'm not going to go with you anymore," she said. "I don't care what you say."

"Okay," said Mama. She smiled and reached out to wipe off some tears Meggie had missed.

Just then the phone rang. Mama and Meggie looked at each other and waited.

"Ma!" Reenie called. "It's Sam!"

"Oh, no!" they said.

Mama smiled and got to her feet. "I'll be rewarded for this someday, right?"

EIGHT

Grape season came in late September. It was Meggie's favorite. She ate the grapes one by one, right out of the kettle. One by one because of the seeds, but also because of the skins. The skins were where the flavor was. She had a technique. Break the skin with your teeth, then slip the greenish fruit out and eat it, spitting the seeds at the nearest sister. Then savor the skin. While the very outside was chewy and bitter, the rich purple pulp that clung to the inside was sweet and full of flavor.

When Sam called and Mama brought home the first batch of the year, Meggie couldn't wait to dig in.

"Meggie," Mama said, "save some for the jam!"

"There's a whole potful," Meggie said. She bit into a grape.

Just then, as though they could smell the fruit, Lissa and Reenie came into the kitchen. "Grapes!" Reenie said. Lissa grabbed a handful.

"Girls!" Mama said.

"I was reading about how in Italy they used to stomp on grapes with their feet to make wine," Reenie said. "Can we try it? We'll wash our feet first."

"Ew," said Lissa. "I'm not going to step in a bunch of grapes. And then eat them? Gross."

"Cool!" Meggie said, spitting a seed at Lissa, who scowled darkly. "Can we, Mama? Please?"

Mama sighed. "Outdoors," she said. "And don't you dare step one foot inside this house until you've rinsed every bit of juice off your feet!"

They picked out the sticks and leaves and dumped the grapes into the big tin wash bucket

Meggie dragged up from the basement and cleaned with the hose.

Reenie got a pail and filled it with hot soapy water. They sat down on the sidewalk and scrubbed their feet.

"Me first," said Reenie. "I'm the oldest."

"Yeah," said Meggie. "Age before beauty."

Reenie stuck out her tongue and climbed into the bucket. Her feet and ankles turned purple as the juice squeezed out of the grapes.

Then it was Meggie's turn. The grapes felt cool and slimy. Seeds slid between her toes. She had to hold on to Reenie to keep from falling. Lissa watched from the porch with a frown on her face.

"I'm not going to eat anything made from that stuff," she said. "It'll probably smell like feet."

Mama took pictures, and then she helped them rinse their feet with the icy cold water from the hose. But no matter how hard they rubbed, they couldn't get the purple out. Meggie would have to wear dark knee socks for the next

three days to hide her stained feet and ankles. It was worth it, though, she thought.

Mama strained out the seeds and skins and made a grape chiffon pie from the juice. The pie had never tasted so scrumptious, Meggie thought. Even Lissa broke down and ate some. "You would never know it had feet in it," she said.

When they told Papa about the grape stomping, he wrinkled his nose and said, "I hope you washed them first."

"The grapes?" Meggie asked.

"No, silly," he said, "your feet."

"Oh, yes," Meggie said, "we washed them first."

"In that case," said Papa, "may I have a second piece of pie, please?"

NINE

That fall there was a freezer full of grape juice and wild berries, and the pantry shelves were lined with jars of jam and jelly. It was all delicious, but still, Meggie thought, she would rather have store-bought jam like everyone else and not have to put up with Old Sam.

Once it got cold, the family didn't see him much, except at church. And then the girls did a pretty good job of avoiding him with their bathroom technique. Meggie still felt guilty, but she decided that was better than actually having to talk to Old Sam. When Mama had him come over to split firewood, Meggie hid in her bedroom.

In November he went off on his cruise to see some eclipse somewhere, so they didn't have to think about him at all. It seemed strange to Meggie that he could afford to travel all over the world but couldn't find a better place to live.

"I guess traveling is more important to him," Mama said.

Meggie remembered going to his room with Mama once to bring him food. Old Sam had been sick.

"Why doesn't he just cook something himself?" Meggie had asked.

"He doesn't have a stove," Mama had said.

Most of the time, Old Sam ate at different sandwich shops in town. He'd go to one until the manager told him not to come back because he bothered the customers. Then he'd switch to another one. Now and then, he'd call Mama and tell her to talk to one of the restaurant managers and convince him to let Sam eat there again. Mama always did. "He's got to eat somewhere," she'd say.

His room was dark and dirty, and it smelled strongly of Old Sam. The only furniture was a small bed, a bureau, and a chair. The white sheets on the bed were so dirty, they were brown in the middle where he lay down every night. But there were books everywhere. They were piled on the bureau and on the chair. They were piled in the corners and under the bed. About astronomy mostly, Meggie had noticed. And philosophy, Mama had pointed out.

"What's philosophy?" Meggie asked Mama later.

"It's thinking about big questions," Mama said. "About love and about how people live and why they die."

Meggie thought about that for a minute. Then she said, "And about how a little boy named Sam could grow up to be a crazy old berry-picking man?"

Mama put her hand on Meggie's head and brushed her bangs back from her face. She smiled. "Yes, Meggie," she said, "about things like that."

Meggie loved the weeks just after Thanksgiving and before Christmas. Downtown was all lit up, and on the first Sunday in December, they went caroling with a group from church at the houses of the people they knew who were shut in. Meggie and Jolene walked together. Afterward, the carolers went to Meggie's house. The woodstove in the kitchen crackled and hissed, and they stood around it until their fingers and toes thawed. Then the kids went downstairs and played games and drank hot chocolate.

Mama always made a big deal about decorating the house. It used to be that everyone helped, but now that Meggie's sisters were older, they didn't have time to hang lights in the windows and ornaments on the tree. And Papa was never much for helping, though he had done it when they were little because Mama would frown and tell him, "Christmas is for family." After a while, she didn't even have to say anything, just give him that raised-eyebrow look. It became kind of a family joke—Christmas is for family.

Meggie and Mama did all the decorating themselves. Meggie didn't miss her sisters one bit. Especially Lissa, who had a way of taking the fun out of everything. Why she couldn't enjoy Christmas like a normal person, Meggie didn't understand. But she couldn't. And it wasn't only Christmas. It was everything. Meggie wondered if Lissa wanted to be miserable. That seemed like a weird choice. Or maybe it wasn't a choice. Maybe she couldn't help herself. Like Old Sam, Meggie thought. He didn't choose to be the way he was, she figured. He just was.

When the decorating was done, Meggie started on her Christmas projects. Making presents for people was her passion. She loved looking in magazines for pictures that fit someone's personality and gluing them together to tell a story about that person.

This year she was pasting the pictures onto

picture frames. She'd bought a bunch of cheap wooden ones at the craft store. "People will have to find their own photographs to put in them," she told Mama, "since I don't have a camera."

TEN

Shortly before Christmas, Meggie was upstairs working on her picture frames when the phone rang. She waited for someone to answer it, but after five rings, she ran to get it. Her fingers were covered with glue.

"Hello?" she said.

"Nan?"

She almost dropped the phone. Old Sam never called this time of year! She wanted to hang up on him. But she didn't.

"Mama!" she shouted. Her mother came to the phone wrapped in a towel. She was dripping from the bath. "It's Sam," Meggie whispered, her hand over the receiver. Mama grimaced and took the phone. A puddle was forming at her feet.

That's a picture, thought Meggie.

"Hello, Sam," Mama said . . . "Christmas?" she asked.

It was Meggie's turn to grimace. She knew what he wanted. He wanted to come for Christmas dinner.

"Well, I don't know," Mama said. She looked at Meggie, who was shaking her head frantically.

"Uh-huh," Mama said. "Uh-huh," she said again. Then she said, "I'll have to let you know, Sam."

Meggie could hear Sam slam the phone down on the other end. Mama groaned.

"He'll ruin everything," Meggie said.

"He usually goes to Reverend Wallace's house," Mama explained, as though Meggie didn't already know that. "But she just had the baby, and she's not up to it this year."

Meggie stared at her mother. She couldn't believe she was even considering it.

"I understand how you feel," Mama said, "but he doesn't have anywhere else to go."

Meggie didn't know why, but she was feeling stubborn. Maybe it was because she had to put up with Old Sam the rest of the year—she wasn't going to let that crazy old berry-picking man spoil her Christmas.

"Please, Mama," she begged. "Can't he go to the soup kitchen or something? Christmas is for family, remember?"

Mama sighed. "What am I going to say?"

But the next Sunday in church, Mama told Old Sam he couldn't come for Christmas.

"Why not?" he said.

Mama turned red and looked at her feet. "It just wouldn't work out," she said.

Old Sam didn't say anything.

Meggie hid in the girls' room. Her stomach hurt.

The night before Christmas, the phone rang. It was snowing hard. Meggie was in the living room, looking at all the presents under the tree and wondering which ones were for her. There was a fire in the fireplace, and it was warm and cozy in front of the tree. Millicent was purring loudly in her lap.

Besides a camera, Meggie had asked for new skates this year, bright white ones with no cartoon characters on them. Grown-up skates like her sisters had, which hadn't already been worn so much by both of them that her ankles turned inward. Then maybe they'd let her go to the pond with them.

She frowned, remembering the last time she went skating. Her sisters and their friends were playing crack-the-whip. "You have to be on the end," Lissa had said, "because you're the smallest." When she'd gone flying and smacked her knees on the ice, they'd all laughed. Reenie had had to help her home. Her knees were purple and sore for a week. With new skates, maybe she'd be able to stay on her feet better. She would look less like a baby, anyway.

She heard Mama hang up the phone. She

didn't say goodbye. Old Sam, Meggie thought, the ache returning to her stomach.

Mama came into the room. Her arms were crossed in front of her. Meggie wondered if her stomach hurt, too.

"Meggie," Mama said, "Sam's been hurt."

"What happened?"

"He was hitchhiking, trying to get to the Sharptons' house for Christmas. He was hit by a car. I guess the driver didn't see him, or couldn't stop. At any rate, Sam's leg is broken."

Meggie felt as though she was going to throw up. It was her fault. If she'd said he could come for Christmas dinner, he wouldn't have been out in the storm.

"What are you going to do?" she asked Mama.

"I'm going to the hospital," Mama said. "I'll see what his doctor says. I don't know as there's much else I can do. He wants me to come get him."

"Can you get him?" Meggie asked. "I mean, doesn't he need to stay in the hospital?"

"I guess that will be up to his doctor," Mama

said. She was pulling on her winter coat and boots.

Meggie thought about Sam hurt and alone in the hospital. "Can I go with you?" she asked.

Mama looked up, surprised. "Sure," she said. "Get your coat. It's cold out there."

Meggie went to the closet and got her jacket. She put on her boots and her hat and mittens. She followed Mama to the car, and they rode in silence to the hospital.

ELEVEN

It was wet and raw outside. The fluffy white snow was turning to cold gray rain. Christmas lights that had seemed so bright were dim and dismal in the gloom. The sidewalks and roads were deep with slush. Meggie imagined Sam lying hurt in the slush, waiting for the ambulance. She shivered.

At the hospital, they walked down the hall to Old Sam's room. Their wet boots squeaked on the polished linoleum floor. Christmas carols were playing softly on the radio at the nurses' station. The plastic Santas and fake greenery looked cheap and ugly in the harsh hospital light.

"Here we are," Mama said when they reached Old Sam's room.

"Is that you, Nan?" Old Sam called from his bed.

"Yes, Sam," Mama said. Meggie followed her into the room. "How are you?"

"Terrible," said Old Sam. He sounded angry. "I want to go home," he said. "I want you to take me home."

"I can't do that, Sam," Mama said. "You can't take care of yourself in this condition."

"I'll die if I stay here," Old Sam told her. "I don't want to die in a hospital."

Mama took his hand and looked at Meggie helplessly. Meggie remembered what Mama had said, that Old Sam had lived in a hospital for twenty-five years.

"You've got to take me home," Old Sam said again, and he started to cry.

He looked small and frightened, lying in that clean white hospital gown, on that clean white hospital bed. Meggie's stomach hurt more than ever. She looked at the floor, the window, the

gold tinsel star on the door—anywhere but at Old Sam.

Mama told Old Sam a couple more times that she couldn't take him home. Then she and Meggie said goodbye, and Mama went to look for his doctor.

While Mama was talking to the doctor, Meggie thought about Old Sam. He hadn't called her Heidi today. He hadn't said she was his favorite child. He hadn't tried to pat her face with his rough berry-picking fingers. He had just held Mama's hand and cried.

"Well," said Mama, "the doctor says Sam could go home tomorrow if there were someone to take care of him. His niece can't travel so far."

"So there isn't anyone," Meggie said.

"No," said Mama. She took Meggie's hand, and they walked out of the hospital.

It was dark outside, and still drizzling. The wind was blowing cold, and a thin layer of ice was beginning to cover everything.

"Poor old soul," Mama said. "What a way to spend Christmas."

"It's my fault," Meggie said.

"What?" Mama sounded surprised. "It's no one's fault, Meggie," she said. "It was an accident."

Maybe so, but Meggie couldn't stop thinking about Old Sam. She thought about him all the way home. She thought about Christmas. She thought about presents and Christmas trees and fires in the fireplace. She thought about Christmas morning and Papa's special tree-shaped coffee cake. And she thought about peanut butter and cheese and pickle and jelly sandwiches. She was still thinking when she went to bed.

In the morning, Meggie got up early and went into Mama and Papa's room.

Papa groaned. "It's too early for presents. Go back to bed."

"I have to talk to you about something," Meggie said, crawling over Papa to take up the middle of the bed.

Mama sighed and turned on the light. "It's five o'clock in the morning," she said, squinting at the alarm clock on her dresser.

"I know," Meggie said. "I couldn't sleep. I was thinking about Old Sam."

Papa groaned again and rolled over.

Mama said, "Old Sam? What about him?"

"I was thinking it's not right for him to spend Christmas in the place he hates more than anything," Meggie said. "I think we should bring him here for Christmas dinner."

Mama smiled and put her arm around Meggie. "I think you're right," she said, and kissed her on the top of her head.

"But Christmas is for family," Papa said.

Mama and Meggie both clobbered him with pillows.

"All right, all right," he hollered, laughing. "I'll go get him after breakfast!"

TWELVE

Papa went out right after coffee cake.

"Where's he going?" Lissa wanted to know.

"You'll see," Meggie said. She smiled at Mama, and Mama smiled back.

After a while, Papa came home with Old Sam in a wheelchair. Lissa and Reenie moaned. "Mama," Reenie said, "it's Christmas."

"Precisely," Mama said.

Meggie looked out the window. Papa was wheeling Old Sam up to the house. It was hard going because of the ice, and now it was snowing again.

Sam was cursing loudly by the time Papa had

helped him up the porch stairs and into the kitchen. Papa sat him at the table with his leg propped up and went back out for the wheelchair.

Meggie could feel the coffee cake beginning to swirl in her stomach. Reenie and Lissa glared at her. Meggie didn't blame them. Christmas was ruined, and it was all her fault.

"Merry Christmas, Sam," Mama said, trying hard—too hard—to sound cheerful.

"My leg hurts," Sam grumbled. "I'm hungry!"

"Can I get you some coffee cake?" Mama asked.

Sam scowled. "Coffee," he said. "Black. And eggs. Scrambled. With cheese. And hot sauce."

What, no pickles? Meggie thought. But she didn't say it. "I'll help, Mama," she said.

Sam looked at her as though he'd just noticed she was there. "Heidi," he said. His voice softened and he reached out his hand toward her, then dropped it back into his lap.

Meggie smiled, but she didn't move. "Merry Christmas, Sam," she said. "I'm just going to get your eggs." She forced out another smile and went to the fridge. "How many do you want, Sam?" she asked.

"Six," Sam said. Then he said, "Heidi," again.

There was a sad tenderness in his voice, and Meggie felt as though somehow he understood why she hid when he was around, and that perhaps he forgave her. She broke the eggs into a bowl and beat them with a fork. Lissa grated some cheese, and Reenie dug around in the cabinet for the hot sauce.

Mama poured the coffee and set it in front of Sam.

While the eggs cooked, Meggie watched Old Sam drink his coffee. They'd cleaned him up at the hospital, shaved his cheeks and washed his glasses. Somehow he'd even gotten clean clothes, though the trousers were cut up the side to make room for his cast. Sitting there, he looked almost like a little boy.

Meggie scooped the eggs from the pan onto a plate and sprinkled them with hot sauce. Old Sam picked up his fork and began shoveling the eggs into his mouth as though he hadn't eaten in months.

"More hot sauce," he said.

Reenie handed him the bottle, and he shook it over the eggs. Meggie's mouth burned just from looking at those eggs drenched in pepper sauce. It occurred to her for the first time that maybe Old Sam's taste buds were the only part of him that were allowed to feel anything. No wonder he wanted everything to have as much flavor as possible.

"Do you want some pickles, Sam?" she asked him. He nodded. She got the jar of dill pickles out of the refrigerator and put them on the table.

Sam dug one out with his fingers, splashing pickle juice on his eggs. Reenie and Lissa made gagging faces at each other. Mama frowned at them.

"Heidi," Old Sam said, gazing up at her. Then to Mama, "She's my favorite child."

"She's a good girl, isn't she, Sam?" Mama said.

THIRTEEN

After breakfast, Old Sam sat in his wheelchair in the living room and watched them open their presents. Meggie got a couple of puzzles in her stocking, which he figured out in no time. She wondered if he ever wished he'd gone to college. His brother had. She knew because Old Sam had told Mama about him once. He was a genius, too, and had gone to college when he was fourteen or something.

Papa handed out the presents under the tree one by one. Meggie wished there were something for Old Sam, but there hadn't been time. Besides, what do you get for a crazy old man?

Meggie opened the only big box with her

name on it. Skates. They were shiny and white, and the blades glinted in the light from the Christmas tree. They came with rubber guards for the blades so she could walk on the floor of the warming hut without dulling them. They were beautiful. They really were. But they weren't a camera.

She tried not to let her disappointment show. Mama had said she couldn't have a camera of her own until she was old enough to take care of it. "A camera is not a toy." Still, Meggie had hoped Mama would think she was old enough this year.

"Thanks," she said, holding up the skates. "They're great."

From Reenie there was a poster of a cat that looked just like Millicent. And from Lissa there was a six-pack of nail polish. Meggie looked at her raw fingertips and wondered whether her sister knew her at all.

Reenie smiled when she opened the frame Meggie had made. Lissa didn't say anything when she opened hers. She just tossed her ponytail over her shoulder and whispered something to Reenie. After all that work, Meggie thought, remembering the hours up in her room choosing the right pictures and pasting them on the frame, she doesn't even like it. She slumped back against the wall and sighed.

Old Sam fell asleep for a while and snored loudly. "The doctors put him on medication for the pain in his leg," Mama said, "so he may not be himself."

"Good," said Lissa. Meggie tossed one of her pairs of new Christmas socks and hit her sister in the head.

———————

Jolene called in the afternoon. She loved her frame. "I'm going to put that picture in it. You know, the one of you and me on the swing."

"The one from when we were three?" Meggie laughed. That was her favorite picture. She and Jo had been playing dress-up. Meggie was wearing a pink tutu and a crazy wig made with strips of shiny plastic in bright colors. Jo had a blue tutu with sequins, and she was wearing an old black hat. They were playing on the swing when Jo's mother came along and took their picture. "It'll look great in there," she said, and laughed again.

Then Meggie told Jo about Old Sam's accident.

"Oh," Jo said. "That's terrible. But I can't believe you invited him to dinner!"

"Neither can I," Meggie said. "But it's not so bad," she added, surprising herself. "He's just kind of a lonely old man. Besides, they gave him a bath and clean clothes at the hospital."

She was starting to see things the way Mama did, she thought. She didn't have to like Old Sam to care about his feelings. She heard Mama's voice in her head. Shadow and light. Shades of gray. Even Old Sam wasn't black and white. He was a lot more complicated than that.

FOURTEEN

Christmas dinner was fit for royalty. "Unfortunately," Papa said later, "we only had Old Sam."

He wouldn't eat the turkey, of course, because he was a vegetarian, or the stuffing, since it had oysters in it. He took mountains of mashed potatoes and squash and creamed onions, and dumped sweet gherkins all over them. But the worst part was when he piled green olives on Mama's Christmas cheesecake. Mama didn't mind, but it didn't improve anyone else's appetite. Table manners still weren't one of Old Sam's strong suits.

After dinner, when Papa said he had to take

Sam back to the hospital, Sam cried. "I'll die," he said. "I won't go. They'll kill me."

He turned to Mama. "Please, Nan," he begged. "Can't I stay here? I won't be any trouble. Please?"

"No, Sam," Mama said. "You need to be where someone can take care of you." She took his hand. "We're glad you could come and share Christmas with us, though."

"I hate hospitals," Sam said.

"I know, Sam," said Mama.

"I can't eat anything," he said. "I'll die."

"You'll be all right," Mama said. "You'll be better soon. Then you can go home."

Sam shook his head sadly all the way to the car. Papa helped him get in and put the wheelchair in the trunk. Meggie watched from the window. She felt awful. Maybe it would have been better if they had left him in the hospital for Christmas. Then he wouldn't have to face going back.

"It's too sad, Mama," she said, turning away.

"It would have been sadder if he'd had to spend the day in the hospital," said Mama.

Papa was walking around to the driver's side when Meggie had an idea. She went to the pantry and took a jar off the shelf. Then she ran to the car and opened the door. She handed the jar to Old Sam. He looked up at her with wet eyes. "Heidi," he said.

"Pickles," she said. "For the hospital food."

Sam didn't say anything, but he held the jar close to his chest.

"Merry Christmas," Meggie said. She was about to shut the door when Lissa came out carrying something.

Lissa reached into the car and handed it to Old Sam. It was the frame Meggie had made for her. She had put in a picture of Meggie and Reenie stomping grapes. "You can make me another one," Lissa whispered as she ran back into the house.

Meggie smiled. So that was what she'd been talking to Reenie about.

As Papa started down the driveway, Old Sam

turned back and looked at Meggie. He put his fingers to his lips and blew her a kiss. She smiled and waved, then walked back into the house.

Mama was standing in the kitchen with a beat-up leather satchel in her hands. She held it out to Meggie. "You haven't opened this yet," she said.

Meggie took the case. She didn't have to open it. It was her grandfather's camera, the old silver Nikon he'd gotten in Japan when he was in the service. It was the camera her mother had learned on.

"No bells and whistles," Mama said. "Just you and the light and the shadows."

Meggie put the case on the table and sprung the catch. The camera glistened through her tears.

Mama put her arms around Meggie and held her close. "I'm proud of you," she said. "It was very grown up of you to share your Christmas with Sam."

Meggie choked down the lump in her throat. "Thanks," she said. She picked up the camera and held it to her eye. "It's beautiful."

"Hey, Meggie," Lissa said, "Reenie and I are going skating. Want to come?"

Through the viewfinder, she saw her sister's face was half in daylight, half in shadow.

"No crack-the-whip," Lissa said.

"Promise?" Meggie said.

"Promise," Lissa said. "And when we get back, I'll do your nails."

Meggie held out her hands and tried to picture her nails painted pink. It occurred to her that she hadn't bitten them all day.

She looked at her mother. She felt guilty about running off after Mama had given her such a special present, but Mama was grinning. "Go ahead," she said. "We'll have plenty of time to practice with the camera."

"Yeah," said Lissa, striking a beauty-queen pose. "And you've got the perfect subject!"

Meggie laughed. Carefully she returned the

camera to the case and went to grab her skates. She couldn't remember the last time her sister had clowned around with her. She smiled. Christmas had turned out pretty well, after all.